Hide and Ghost Seek

A HIDDEN PICTURE COUNTING BOOK

A Grosset & Dunlap **ALL ABOARD BOOK®**

Library of Congress Cataloging-in-Publication Data

Thompson, Carol.
   Hide and ghost seek : a hidden picture counting book / by Carol Thompson :
illustrated by Margaret A. Hartelius.
      p.   cm. — (All aboard books)
   Summary: Count to 20, or even 150, while searching out the ghosts hidden
throughout the town, from ghoul school to monster market.
   [1. Ghosts—Fiction.   2. Stories in rhyme.   3. Counting.]
I. Hartelius. Margaret A., ill.   II. Title.   III. Series.
PZ8.3.T3195Hi 1992 [E]—dc20 91-33999 CIP AC
ISBN 0-448-40475-3

Hide and Ghost Seek
A HIDDEN PICTURE COUNTING BOOK

By Carol Thompson

Illustrated by Margaret A. Hartelius

Grosset & Dunlap, Publishers

Ghost Town

Monsters shopping! Zombies stopping!
Take a look, this town is hopping!
And look who's hiding—without a doubt,
There's one ghost inside, two ghosts out!

Find
1
ghost!

Ghoul School

"Who's that yelling?" "Hey, I'm telling!"
Hear the witches practice spelling.
Three little ghosts are in this room,
And four are hiding near the witches' brooms!

A B C D E F G H I J K L M N O P

Abracadabra
Shazaa
Ishka

LUNCH FOR
TODAY
Spook-ghetti
Boo-looney
sandwitches
Boo-berries

Find
3
ghosts!

Find
4
ghosts!

A Favorite Haunt

Ice cream dripping! Best fiends sipping!
See the fresh cream get a whipping!
Sy is spinning on a stool,
And five hidden ghosts are feeling cool!

Out-of-this-World Series

Igor pitches! The hitter switches!
Watch the Ghouls strike out the Witches!
Six little ghosts enjoy this inning.
See them grinning? Their team's winning!

| VISITORS | 0 | 1 | 0 | 6 | 0 | 0 | | |
| HOME | 0 | 0 | 4 | 2 | 13 | | | |

STIFF STUFF NEW! IMPROVED! scare spray

BUY Second Sight Spook-tacles

Spook-Plugs checked at Igor's Gar...

Find 6 ghosts!

Boo Plate Special

"Some blood-red punch?" "Thanks a bunch!"
"Harry, please don't wolf your lunch!"
The ghouls and boys go out to eat,
And seven ghosts wait for a seat.

Hot Ghost Beef Platter
Hungarian Ghoul-ash
Scream of Tomato Soup

Boo-berry Pie

Find **7** ghosts!

Stars of the Silver Scream

Popcorn's flying! The baby's crying!
Monster flicks are horrifying!
If you get scared and close your eyes,
Eight ghosts will take you by surprise!

Find **8** ghosts!

Monster Market

"What a great price!" "Isn't this nice?"
"Please, Mummy, let me buy these mice!"
The monsters love a close-out sale,
And nine ghosts go on the bargain trail.

Wash and Scare

Come make the scene, shrink your jeans,
And play with the purple change machine!
The monsters' clothes look clean and neat,
And ten tidy ghosts can wash their sheets!

Swimming Ghouls

Suntan lotion? What a notion!
Monsters cause a beach commotion!
Slim Bones's kids have buried him,
And eleven ghosts get in the swim!

Find **11** ghosts!

A Spook-tacular Show

Let's give a cheer! The rock band's here!
Their music shakes the chandelier!
Twelve hidden ghosts are having a ball.
Look carefully and you'll find them all!

EXIT

Find
12
ghosts!

Scary Fair

Be brave! Beware! Hold on to your hair!
Come ride the rides at the monster fair!
Igor is spinning through the air,
And thirteen ghosts are in for a scare!

BAT FUN HOUSE

SCARY·GO·ROUND

Find **13** ghosts!

Traveling Ghost to Ghost

Jubilation at the station!
Monsters going on vacation!
Fourteen ghosts are traveling, too.
They're on their way to Mali-boo!

Unearthly Birthday

Burgers and franks! Birthday spanks!
Perfectly monstrous presents—thanks!
Eating too much devil's food cake
Gives fifteen ghosts a stomachache!

Scare Bear

STINKER TOYS

Find **15** ghosts!

Scary, Scary Night

"Tell a story!" "Make it gory!"
This is monster terror-tory!
The campers love a scary tale.
But twenty ghosts are turning pale!

Find
20
ghosts!

Have you found all the ghosts hiding in this book?
If you don't think you have, then take another look.
Search every picture for ghosts big and small.
If you count 150, then you've found us all!